A GRIFFIN IN THE GARDEN

by Elsa Marston • pictures by Larry Daste

TAMBOURINE BOOKS • NEW YORK

Library of Congress Cataloging in Publication Data

Marston, Elsa. A griffin in the garden/by Elsa Marston;
pictures by Larry Daste.—1st ed. p.cm.
Summary: Gregory's attempt to turn his backyard into a rock
garden is thwarted by a griffin that arrives one stormy night
and does not want to leave.
[1. Griffins—Fiction.]   I. Daste, Larry, ill.   II. Title.
PZ7.M356755Gr1993 [E]—dc20 92-35399 CIP AC
ISBN 0-688-10981-0.—ISBN 0-688-10982-9 (lib. bdg.)
1   3   5   7   9   10   8   6   4   2
FIRST EDITION

For my son Ramsay
...may your gardens grow
E.M.

For Laura

L.D.

Gregory dug and dug in his backyard, until he had a good deep hole and a huge pile of dirt. He wanted to make a rock garden and a water lily pool to surprise his mother when she got back from her trip. His father thought that was a fine idea.

The April rains turned the hole into a pool. Meanwhile, Gregory looked for rocks. But there weren't many rocks around. At last he found some broken cinder blocks and bathroom tiles. He stuck them in the pile of dirt and thought they looked pretty nice.

Now all Gregory had to do was plant flowers and help them grow, so the garden would be beautiful for his mother.

But that night a terrible storm blew up. In the morning, Gregory looked out to see if the rock garden was all right.

There, flopped among the cinder blocks, lay a creature with the head of an eagle and paws like a lion's. Its long, tufted tail dangled in the pool, and the feathers on its big golden wings were all cockeyed.

"Hey, Dad, look!" Gregory called.

"Well, what do you know!" said his dad. "A griffin."

"It looks pretty tired," said Gregory. "I'll take it something to eat."

He carried out a large bowl of Rice Krispies. The griffin gobbled them eagerly.

"That's better," it said, sitting up to preen its feathers. There was a strange smell about the griffin, like hot tar and overcooked broccoli.

"Are you all right?" asked Gregory.

The griffin let out a long wheeze. Its breath was quite hot, and Gregory had to step back a bit. "I'm awful tired," said the griffin in a pitiful way. "I got lost in the storm last night, and this was the only mountainous lair I could find. Besides, I hurt myself." It held out one limp wing.

"You can rest here for a while," said Gregory. He didn't think his rock garden really looked like a mountainous lair, but he was glad to help.

By the end of the day, however, he began to wonder how long the creature planned to lie around on the rock garden. It would be very hard to plant flowers with a griffin there.

So he said, "Maybe you'd like to try someplace else for a change. The city park has a nice lake."

"We'll see," said the griffin with a huge, hot yawn. "Say, what else have you got to eat around here?"

The griffin stayed the next day and the one after that. Gregory fed it all the cereal in the house and all the olives, pickles, and chocolate chip cookies. He even gave it all the Popsicles, ice cream, and frozen pizza, but its breath stayed just as hot.

Every time Gregory tried to ask whether it felt well enough to go
home, the creature would start to talk about something else.

"Nice little place you've got here," it said. "Good home cooking.
Nice rocks, very comfy." Then, lifting its wing, the griffin would
groan. "Oooooh! Aaaargh."

A day or two later, Gregory's dad asked, "How much longer is that griffin going to be around?"

"It hasn't said," Gregory answered. "I don't really think it's all that sick, but I don't want to hurt its feelings."

"Well," said his dad with a sigh, "do what you think best."

Gregory called the animal shelter. "There's a griffin on my rock garden," he told the lady who answered the phone, "and I don't know if my mom would like it."

"A griffin?" said the lady. "Well, don't worry, honey, it'll fly away soon. Griffins never hang around too long."

"It says its wing is hurt," Gregory explained. "But I'm not so sure. It has a good appetite."

"Try feeding it onion bagels," she said. "They're on sale this week."
Gregory thanked her, hung up, and sighed.

Suddenly he heard a loud racket in the backyard. Two dogs had squeezed under the gate and were barking at the griffin. That gave Gregory an idea. He pushed the gate wide open, and soon all the dogs in the neighborhood came trotting in. They pranced around the griffin, yipping and yapping, yowling and howling.

After a while the griffin got to its feet and spread its wings. Gregory, holding his ears, grew hopeful. Surely the griffin was ready to leave now!

Then a dreadful noise rose above the dogs' racket—like an eagle screaming and a lion roaring at the same time. It was the griffin, laughing.

A moment later the dogs had all scattered in terror. The griffin lay down again. It looked very pleased with itself.

That night there was a beautiful full moon. After a good supper of corn chips and cupcakes, the griffin began to sing. It sang and sang, in a voice like a catbird gargling. The backyard got very warm.

"I think the griffin is feeling better now," said Gregory.

"Let's hope so," said his dad wearily.

Meanwhile, the neighbors' cats all hurried over. They sat down and meowed and meowed along with the griffin. People came to their windows and back fences and threw shoes, onions, and transistor radios to make them stop singing. But it didn't do any good.

The next morning Gregory had to take all the shoes and radios back to the neighbors. The griffin ate the onions and lay down for a nap.

Gregory sat on the back step, gazing in despair at his rock garden. The griffin was spread all over it, sound asleep, smelling like scorched broccoli and burned onions. The very next day, Gregory's mother was coming home. All she would see was a big pile of dirt and cinder blocks with a fat, lazy griffin on top. That wouldn't be much of a welcome-home present for her.

Gregory decided he had been polite long enough. He marched over to the snoring griffin, grabbed its tail, and yanked as hard as he could.

"Wake up, griffin, wake up!"

The griffin lifted its head sleepily. "Why?"

"Because," yelled Gregory, "I'm trying to make this into a rock garden for my mother! A *garden*, you grabby, ungrateful guest, not a mountainous lair!"

"Oh!" said the griffin, blinking. "A garden? *Not* a mountainous lair? Well, my goodness, why didn't you say so?"

It sat up, wiggled, and sprang into the pool with a splendid splash. There it stayed, lolling in the warm water, while Gregory planted things until night time.

"There, it's done!" said Gregory at last, all worn out. "But nothing will grow in time for Mom, thanks to you." He stomped off into the house.

"Oh," said the griffin, "we'll see." It took a deep breath and let out a great steamy swoosh, which made the whole backyard as warm as a hothouse.

When Gregory's mother came home, there were flowers blooming all over the rock garden and the pool was full of water lilies.

"Why, it's beautiful, Gregory!" she said. "And what a cute statue you've put on top."

Gregory caught the griffin's eye as it perched among the snapdragons and cinder blocks. The griffin winked, and Gregory winked back.

The next morning, it was gone.

"I suppose," said Gregory, "the griffin really had to get home to its own mountainous lair."

"Oh, it'll be back someday," said his dad. "With all its friends. They'll probably want a garden party."

"That would be fun," said Gregory. Then he thought it over.

"But I guess we'd better not ask them to stay for supper."